For Steph. Nice marmot.
–P.M.

To my grandparents and all the fun times we had at the beach.
Thanks, Margaret, Nicole, and Chelsea. And a special thanks to Theo.
–V.V.

Bob and Joss Get Lost!
Text copyright © 2017 by Peter McCleery
Illustrations copyright © 2017 by Vin Vogel
All rights reserved. Manufactured in China.
No part of this book may be used or reproduced in any manner whatsoever
without written permission except in the case of brief quotations embodied in critical articles and reviews.
For information address HarperCollins Children's Books, a division of HarperCollins Publishers,
195 Broadway, New York, NY 10007.
www.harpercollinschildrens.com

Library of Congress Control Number: 2015958389
ISBN 978-0-06-241531-8 (trade bdg.)

The artist used Adobe Photoshop to create the digital illustrations for this book.
Design by Chelsea C. Donaldson
16 17 18 19 20   SCP   10 9 8 7 6 5 4 3 2 1
❖
First Edition

BOB and JOSS

Get Lost!

by Peter McCleery • illustrated by Vin Vogel

HARPER

An Imprint of HarperCollinsPublishers

Bob was bored.

"I'm bored," he said. "Let's do something."

"Let's take a boat trip," said Joss.

"No way," said Bob.

"Why not?" asked Joss.

BOAT RENTALS

"We will get lost," said Bob.

"We won't get lost," said Joss.

They got lost.

"We are lost!" cried Bob.

"We can't be lost," said Joss. "I know where I am."

"You do?"

"Yes," said Joss. "I'm here on a boat with you."

"Is—is that a storm cloud?" asked Bob.

"No," said Joss. "That doesn't look like a storm."

"Oh, thank goodness!" said Bob.

"It looks more like a bunny," said Joss.

"And that one looks like a sheep."

It was not a sheep. It was a storm.

"Bob?" said Joss.
"Yes, Joss?" said Bob.

"Your name is very appropriate right now."
"Indeed," said Bob.

Bob and Joss washed up on an empty beach.

"This island is deserted," declared Bob.

"Deserted? Mmmmm, sounds yummy!" said Joss.

THERE!
THERE IS THE
MONSTER!

AHH! AHHHHHHHHH!

Bob quickly got to work on a shelter. "We'll need shelter before nightfall!"

"Mmm-hmm," said Joss.

"What are you doing?" asked Bob. "Aren't you going to help?"

"I'm drinking a milk shake," said Joss. "Coconut!"

"How can you drink a milk shake right now???" asked Bob.

"Easy. Like this!"

SHLUUUURP.

Later . . .

Where have
you been?

Over
there.

"You know what this shelter needs?" asked Joss.

"What?" said Bob.

"More shelter," said Joss.

I hate this place. There's nothing here! No television, no video games, no books, no clocks, no toys, no cars, no paper, no pens, no chairs, no radio, no computers, no bikes, no peanut butter, no jelly. NOTHING!

Yes. Isn't it wonderful?

"Next thing we need to do," said Bob, "is build a fire."

"Mmm-hmmm," said Joss.

"You gather kindling and I'll rub these sticks togeth– Joss! Are you listening?"

"Yes."

"To me?" asked Bob.

"Oh, gosh no," said Joss. "I'm listening to the waves crashing."

"Is it more important than what I'm saying?" asked Bob.

"I don't know," said Joss. "I don't speak Wave."

Later . . .